# Cat Crazy

Written by Kim Bourgeau
Illustrated by Matthew Gonya
Layout by Jack Bourgeau

OpenDyslexic is a new open-sourced font
created to increase readability for readers
with dyslexia
http://dyslexicfonts.com

Everyone can read this font.

For
Mom and Dad
and
June and Art

On Saturday night Granny and Grandpa were sound asleep.

The wooden window blinds started shaking and rattling.

Granny jumped up and turned on the lights!

It was a crazy cat running out of the bedroom.
"Accckkk a CAT!" yelled Granny in a wild voice.

Granny chased the crazy cat down the hallway.

There they were running all over the house in the middle of the night with all the lights on.

Then it got very quiet, she didn't hear a cat anywhere.
She just could not find that crazy cat. So Granny went
back to bed.

She was so freaked out she kept her eyes open all night long.

When Granny got up in the morning she caught a
glimpse of the crazy cat.

So Granny started vacuuming all over the house to chase the crazy cat out of its hiding place.

She looked under beds...

And she looked behind couches...but she couldn't find that crazy cat anywhere!

Then she could hear tin cans rattling!!! It must be in the kitchen!

Granny opened the back door in the kitchen, got her broom

and scared that crazy cat out right into the snow.

How did that crazy cat get in the house anyway?

It must have snuck in the house when Grandpa brought in the recycling box the night before.

On Sunday morning, Grandpa woke up from his restful night's sleep.

"What's all the racket in here?" said Grandpa.

Granny was just about to tell Grandpa about the crazy cat, he looked up in the corner over the cupboards and saw a bat hanging from the ceiling.

Grandpa said, "Was it a bat making all that noise?"

Granny's eyes and mouth opened WIDE and she went
BAT crazy!

The End.

Author Kim Bourgeau lives in Ottawa, Canada.

You can read Kim's other books

"Go to Sleep Kitty"

and

"Duke the Dog"